Magic
in
Errors

First published on Oct 14, 2023 by Sneha Babu
ISBN – 978-93-100-0474-8

Copyright © Sneha Babu, 2023
Edited and typeset by Mozelle Jordan
Cover design by Sidharth Suresh

Printed on demand by Ingramspark

To David Marshall Pitfield

We sat on top of a cliff together, at the edge of everything living; staring down at oblivion. The idea of that jump seemed inviting, anything to escape the crushing weight of the sky. You made the jump, and I did not. And I'll live through both our choices because before diving in, you made sure I'd never see that view again in this lifetime.

Thank you, Marsh

14 July 2023
8:00 a.m.
Aanjaney

Following a siren blazing ambulance, a truckload of policemen arrives at St. Luke's Hospital, with paparazzi meandering outside ever since. As someone's grandmother once said, "The world's going to hell in a handbasket."

"She's got pinpoint pupils and blue skin," Dr. Irwin says, looking over the patient.

"Damn. Another one? This is the third OD this week," Forman says, not bothering to hide his surprise.

"Shut up, Forman. Get Narcan. Hurry."

"Erratic rhythms, apneic at the scene, last BP 80 over 40," Forman informs Dr. Irwin, as they take the patient to the intensive care unit.

The doctor takes a deep breath, cracks a few knuckles, and puts on his gloves and mask.

Thirty-five minutes later, Dr. Irwin comes out of the ICU and makes his way back outside to the front of the hospital to meet the swarming paparazzi and journalists. He walks up to the cameras and with a dramatic pause says, "We couldn't save her."

Soon after the doctor left, relentless journalists surround the officer in charge for a whiff of the juiciest celebrity death in years, and without waiting to hear the answers, they begin firing their questions one by one.

"Inspector Iyer!"

"Aaanjaney! Sir."

"Do you think her substance abuse from the past had caught up to her?"

"What are the coroner's initial findings?"

"Was this a suicide?"

"Why was she lying near railway tracks?"

"I am not entitled to say anything. You'll know once we know, alright? This is a hospital. Have some decency and back the hell off," Aanjaney Iyer, the inspector assigned to this case, says. He would have to answer for that comment, but right now, he doesn't care. Instead, he puts his focus on fighting away the tears threatening to leave his eyes. Everybody knows the legendary Evelyn Charles, the patient who Dr. Irwin just announced didn't make it. But Aanjaney, on the other hand, more than just knew her. Therein lies the problem.

11 July 2023
5:00 p.m.
Raahil

> *Six little monkeys jumping on the bed.*
> *One fell off, and bumped his head.*
> *Momma called the doctor and the doctor said,*
> *"No more monkeys jumping on the bed."*

Raahil sings this nursery rhyme all day, every day. He first heard it while passing by a kindergarten, and the song remained with him ever since. It makes him feel like those kids with nice shoes. He always thinks about how stupid they look wailing for their mommies, but they never, ever look hungry. And, he has always hated them for that.

Raahil, like every other eight-year-old in his colony, earns a living for himself. He sells stickers at railway stations, sometimes pickpocketing the passengers. At the end of the day, he gives all his earnings to Zaydan Bhai and receives his share of the commission. Zaydan Bhai is the most powerful man Raahil knows. He wants to be like him one day so that other kids from the colony would have to give him whatever he asked for, whenever he asked for it.

The lives of people like Raahil revolve around "one day". The sky is always gray in this part of the city, and uncertainty is the only thing he is certain of. However, it's not always so bad. For instance, today, scourging through bottles and plastics in the nearby landfill, Raahil found coins worth twenty rupees. He became so excited that he forgot all about the smell and scary machines.

Raahil reaches the market, smiling and humming, and as he walks proudly toward a vendor, he demands Jalebis.

The vendor takes a good look at the golden-brown-skinned boy in rags, displaying two missing front teeth when he smiles. "I don't do this for charity, boy," he says.

Raahil rolls his eyes. "No, but I do," he replies, and takes the coins out of his pocket.

The vendor gives Raahil the sweets with a sour look on his face. While packing the Jalebis in a newspaper, all he could think of was his best friend's smile when he gives them to her.

A few years ago, a girl named Amina, who has flawless dark skin, frizzy hair, and deep, hazel eyes, ended up moving into the colony with her father. She has the most beautiful nose that reminds

Raahil of a bridge he once saw. They dance together every time it rains, and they share everything they find.

Raahil has never been happier than when he's with her. Neither has Amina when she's with him. To earn her own share, she cooks, cleans, and babysits for fellow colonists, but her father gambles away every rupee she brings in. Raahil dreams of the day he'll marry Amina and live somewhere far, far away. It'll be just them and the rains.

After obtaining the sweets, Raahil continues his day with a profound sense of achievement. Today, he's on his way to the railway station opposite the University. Since it's Friday, he expects his best targets—the youngsters. He prefers naïve and stupid ones, for they believe the world can change and that they can be the ones to change it. But as for him, he's lived long enough to come to terms with the fact that that kind of thinking is nothing but a futile dream.

Even so, he's noticed that people are often way more generous with him when there's terrible news floating around; most of the time it'll be a hunger or rape story that sparks this generosity. For his own good, Raahil wishes these effects lasted more than a day. These people sleep under a roof, without having to worry about the next meal, while he sleeps under the stars, dreaming about food. In a sense, though, he's the one with more freedom, if not more luxury.

Raahil looks at the overcrowded train platform, takes a deep breath, and convokes his puppy-dog demeanor. It's time to sell some stickers.

"Didi, it's just twenty rupees. You look amazing by the way."

"Bhaiya, cool t-shirt. I haven't eaten in a while.
twenty rupees only."

"Aunty, please. Have a look."

"Uncle, I have a variety of cartoons your kid will love."

"Allah will bless you!"

Some push him away. Some smile. Some even offer to buy him food. None buy anything from him, though. But, knowing Zaydan Bhai's temper, Raahil turns them down, and his stomach curses him for it. He knows that if he doesn't earn enough money, Zaydan Bhai will beat him—or worse. The only reason Raahil hasn't been handicapped yet is because of the fact that he is a good liar with a talent for dishonesty.

"Allah will bless you," he shouts again. Raahil doesn't really want to use Allah's name in vain, but he is sure whoever and wherever God is, they will understand.

Raahil once thought that everyone in the world was living in somebody else's brain. Meaning, everyone, including him, was a fragment of somebody else's imagination. He soon abandoned that theory because that made him feel less real. He told himself, *I am Raahil. I am.*

Then, he thought, *maybe divinity is an invisible scale.* He had heard aunties tell their kids stories about Gods and Goddesses. That made him think, what if these gods are people who somehow found a way to push the scale to the maximum. That made everyone God, without the ability to be God. Again, Raahil didn't like that idea because if it were true, there'd be no point in existing. A world without purpose, either good or bad, would be boring.

Another day, he met a man who said there's no God at all. That man said, "The idea of God has been put forth by brilliant minds. Religious books are actually masterpieces by extraordinary writers. Although, their intention was quite simple. The idea of God is hope. And without hope, we are all lost souls." Raahil walked away from that man with his brain running at lightning speeds. He was shocked.

All these theories made Raahil uneasy. But he came to a conclusion after all; God is a moment. For example, he gave his food to a beggar. She smiled at him. He smiled back. That fraction of a second was God. A woman from his colony gave birth to her child. Raahil saw her holding her baby for the first time. That glorious moment was God. His favorite example is the first time he saw Amina. When they held hands, he looked into her eyes, and he swore, that moment right there, felt like God.

Raahil thinks he's the most communal person in the colony. He goes to churches, temples, and mosques. But, only to steal shoes. If he's lucky, he finds a pair that's his size. Else, he sells them to the cobbler down the street. That's the closest he's ever come to religion.

Raahil is so lost in his thoughts that he forgets about the greatest religion of all: money. So, he continues marketing his products at the top of his voice. That's when he sees a skinny boy drop his wallet. Raahil runs and picks it up, peeking inside. There are lots of 2000 rupee notes in it. Raahil has never even seen one before. He stands there, debating with his conscience, but before he can make a decision, someone taps him on the shoulder. It's the skinny boy, except, it isn't actually a boy. It's a girl with hair like a boy's, who's also wearing boy's clothes.

"What do you think you're doing?" she asks.

Raahil takes a moment to look at the skinny boy who's now a girl. She has paintings all over her right arm. He gives her the wallet and says, "I found this. I was about to give it to you when you found me."

She looks at him skeptically.

He pinches his throat and says, "Maa kasam," with the best puppy eyes he can manage.

She sits on a bench nearby and gestures for him to join her. "What's your name?" she asks.

"Raahil."

"How old are you, Raahil?"

"Eight."

She points towards his stickers and says, "I want one."

Raahil is thrilled and excitedly starts showing her everything. When she gives him a 2000 rupee note, he tells her he doesn't have that much change.

"Give me every sticker you have then," she says.

Raahil is speechless. This is unlike any luck he has ever found in a dumpster.

"Are you going to give them to me or not?" she asks, smiling.

There is something about this girl. Her smile is welcoming and contagious, and soon, he finds that they are talking as if they are long-lost friends. He learns that the skinny girl's name is Ayaana, and that she's a twenty-four-year-old musician. She also tells him that the paintings on her arm are called tattoos. She goes on to explain the meaning of each one of them.

Raahil craves more of Ayaana with every passing second. She reminds him of rainbows. He silently prays that she doesn't dissolve into the sky as well. Unfortunately, her train arrives sooner than he expected, hissing and screeching, and bringing his thoughts on Ayaana to a halt.

Raahil quickly gathers all the stickers, frantically searching for a rubber band to tie them up.

He finds a neon-colored, striped hair tie on the bench they were sitting on. It's a beautiful, yet unusual hair tie. *Perfect for Ayaana,* he thinks to himself. He carefully ties everything up and hands the bundle to her, just in time for her to catch her train.

Ayaana leaves with a promise of singing to him the next time they meet. If she keeps her promise, Raahil would have a new friend. If she doesn't, she wouldn't be the first to do so.

15 July 2023
9:00 a.m.
Aanjaney

"Hi, I'm Inspector Iyer. I'm here for the autopsy report," Aanjaney informs the pathologist at St. Luke's hospital, showing his badge.

"Hey!" the pathologist says, hugging him excitedly. Seeing the puzzled expression on his face as she pulls back, she hurriedly says, "We've met before. Don't you remember? I'm Linda. Linda Mathew? We were in school together."

"Umm, I'm sorry... I can't really place you," he says with an apologetic face.

"Well, this is awkward then," she says, nervously laughing while agitatedly fixing her hair. She remembers him vividly; he always wore a sweatshirt that showed off his physique and his laugh was carefree and sweet, and at the same time, sexy. She also remembered that he walked with a slight slant to his shoulders. She has stalked him on social media multiple times since school. She coughs, trying to break the tension and says, "So…. about that report. There are some things I presume you would like to know before I write an official report."

"Yes," Aanjaney's palms start sweating. All of a sudden, his face pales as he slightly sways and holds his stomach.

"Are you alright? Do you need anything? You seem a little…"

"Water… Please."

She scurries to an employee fridge and grabs a bottle of water from it, handing it to him within moments.

He gulps half of the water down in seconds and waits for the sudden nausea to pass. He can feel Linda's eyes on him, and he wills himself to feel better, if not only to avoid any more awkward silence. "It's just the heat," he says after a minute's pause. "Continue Doctor."

"Call me Linda." she says.

"Continue, *Linda,*" Aanjaney says, smiling, completely aware of Linda's flirty tone. Her body language isn't exactly covert, making him really begin to notice her.

"Yes. As you know, Evelyn was brought in from a fatal OD. She suffered a brain hemorrhage due to the drugs she took. But there is something else."

"What is it?" Aanjaney asks, leaning in from intrigue, Linda having his full attention.

"I found a swelling on the back of her skull which is consistent with blunt force trauma. It could be the actual cause of her internal bleeding. When she was brought in with blue skin, it was assumed to be a clear case of OD. It seemed obvious at the time."

"Hmm…" he ponders while looking at the pictures from the report.

"It gets weirder. Look at what I found stuck inside her esophagus." Linda hands him a transparent evidence bag.

"What's this?"

"Looks like an elastic neon hair tie."

"There's no mystery here, Linda. Druggies do all kinds of crazy stuff."

"But the injection marks on her arms are faded, which means she'd been clean for some time. That is wildly inconsistent with the cocktail of drugs we identified on the tox screen. So perhaps, it was involuntary. As for the bump on her head, it is possible she could have accidently tripped and fell, managing to hit her head on a hard object nearby, a rock or even the cement."

"Yes, that seems like a very plausible scenario," he says moving closer to her with every word. "The rumors around town are that no one was surprised to hear she overdosed. She could have wandered off to the railway station in some drug-induced hallucination, tripped and fell, finally ending up here." He is so close to her now that he can hear her heart beating wildly against her chest. His fingertips gently graze her skin. Aanjaney is nervous she'll be offended and ask him to leave.

But she doesn't. Instead, she closes her eyes momentarily, her breathing becoming rapid.

He decides to press his luck further and speaks softly now, his lips touching her ear, "Linda, sweetheart, there's no point of including the hair tie in the report. You know how these people are. Media wants a story. Superiors want to drive my ass. That means a lot more paperwork for both of us. Don't you think?" His thumb slightly brushes her lower lip, and a small moan escapes her body.

His breath falling on her neck exposes all of her carnal desires. He is going to kiss her. He is sure she would let him. But, all of a sudden, to Aanjaney's utmost surprise, she walks away from him. He watches her, amazed as Linda lights a cigarette and takes a nice, long drag. "100000 and we have a deal," she says.

22 August 2020
5:30 p.m.
Evelyn

Evelyn Charles is on a beach, leaning on her lover's shoulder, her face fitting perfectly in the crook of his neck. They look at the horizon in silence. Waves crash on her heart, birthing soft and beautiful ripples. They don't seem to end. Maybe because she doesn't want them to. Maybe because she wants a little forever to claim too.

Evelyn is the kind of girl that wears 'be kind' t-shirts under her black, faux leather jacket and loves hugs more than most people she knows. She hates the movie trope narrating a perfect, manic pixie girl that "isn't like other girls", goes to a Black Lives Matter protest with a strawberry milkshake in hand, and attempts telepathy with her houseplant and dogs. She is miserable during winter months, has no impulse control, and isn't afraid of double texting because *who cares*. She'll tell you she loves you even if you had just met because *why not*.

She is loud, clumsy, and laughs at herself when she falls on her ass, which happens more often than one would think. Evelyn saves popsicle sticks to make castles with her boyfriend. She dances to Taylor Swift and Marvin Gaye. She is everybody's airport crush; the girl people will turn around for, for a second glance.

Yesterday, while her boyfriend was cooking breakfast to their favorite songs and goofing around, she looked at him; the twinkle in his eyes whenever he laughed, and the warmth in his smile when he looked at her. In that moment, she knew. There is nobody she'd rather be with for the rest of her life. So, she turned off the stove, took his hands in hers, looked into his eyes and asked him, "Will you marry me?"

After a night full of tears and arguments, and then finally falling asleep on the floor in each other's arms, here they are, pouring their feelings into the Arabian sea.

"Evy?"

"Hmm?"

"Don't do this to us please. I need you. I need us."

"My point exactly."

"Marriage and family. These things will fuck up everything. They always do. And I don't want to lose you. Why can't we keep going on like this? We are happy, aren't we? I will always be with you. I won't let anything come between us," he says, holding her closer to his chest.

She breaks the embrace and says, "Don't you get it? The only thing coming between us is you. I understand why you hate the idea of having a family. And I am sorry for everything you went through. But we are not your parents. We are different, you and I. We can have a home."

"I cannot give you that," he says, shaking his head. "I just can't."

"Then, we are just wasting our time, aren't we? Delaying the inevitable."

"Don't say that," he begs.

"I have never had a home. You know that. There's nothing I want more. I will never be happy, baby, if we don't take our relationship to the next step. I... I am so sorry," she says, tears brimming her eyes.

"Me too," he says, kissing her with everything he has.

Tears stream down their faces, each one of them hoping the other will stay. They kiss, exchanging unspoken promises, knowing full well this might be their last. Sun rays pierce their heart and the memories come flowing. They keep writing love letters on the sand for the sea to steal them away.

After a moment, Evelyn looks at him, longingly.

"I know," he says, reducing life to that moment. They sit there in comfortable silence, wishing for frozen seconds.

Sailing a million nautical miles away, from the regular and ordinary, they see silence. Stunning and scary, a neat con, by the beautiful. So now, holding hands, they are prepared. Love tossed around by the waves and emotions spiraling down a whirlpool, trust becoming the anchor that fends off a wreck so cruel. Icebergs haunt them and storms prevail, but they promise to keep sailing forever. If the sea kills them, so be it. For once they got a taste of the ocean, there was no going back.

Gazing at the twilight glow, Evelyn realizes endings are as beautiful as the beginnings. The mighty sun drowns in the ocean, boundless like their love, giving its final kiss. His beauty and glow are infinite. But just like this twilight, their love will fade too.

11 July 2023
Raahil

Pigeons. Raahil can't stop staring at their soft necks. So delicate. What would it feel like to hold their necks in his grasp, a tiny, harmless squeeze.

Amina looks at his dazed eyes and smacks him. Every day, without fail, they meet their friend Amir on the rooftop of his house. Amir's family has goats and pigeons, and he goes to the local school. They are rich people. Raahil secretly resents this about him but tolerates him anyway for a chance to look at the pigeons.

Amina, with a mouthful of jalebi, says, "I have to go home now, or else Abbu will be worried."

Raahil, still in a trance from the fragile creatures, doesn't reply.

Amir bids her goodbye and continues to feed the birds. There is suddenly a lot of noise coming from the street. It becomes so loud that Raahil finally snaps out of his daze.

"What's happening down there?" Amir asks, walking closer to the sound of people yelling.

"I have no—"

There is a deafening silence.

Then, Raahil hears a loud ringing and nothing else. His right ear feels wet. He touches it and sees there is blood on his fingertips. Through growing dust and smoke, he sees his friend lying on the ground. He walks towards Amir and finds him, covered in blood and fighting to breathe. Raahil carefully removes each metal shrapnel from his skin. Amir is trying to say something, but the ringing still hasn't stopped in Raahil's ears. After a moment, Amir is finally still.

Raahil shoves the shrapnel into his pockets and slowly walks towards the pigeons.

11 July 2023
7:00 p.m.
Ayaana

That which is unreal, does not exist. That which is real, does not cease to exist. Ayaana Iyer remembers this quote from Bhagwat Geeta, a scripture her mother read to her as a child. Today, she got a taste of something so incredibly real that she did something she's never done before. She made a promise. And, what's more, is she plans on keeping it because Raahil, a complicated slum boy, became her muse today.

In this greedy world, being enough for someone is a magical thing. Just us and our perfect flaws. We are enough and infinite. Sadly, time is neither. So, people are trapped in its webs, with their cardinal crime, their greed, staring back at them. A minute more, they'll pray. A second more, they'll beg. Alas, sin payment is due. So, they whisper a short prayer, "Not now." The definition of enough is different for different people. The simpler it is, the happier they'll be.

Ayaana is a successful musician. She doesn't need to travel by trains and buses, but she does anyway, for the sole purpose of meeting interesting people, like Raahil. She collects stories for her music, and that's why every song she's ever written is so raw and real. Apparently, the Indian Music Academy Awards thinks so too.

Ayaana lives her life as if she could wake up any minute and find out it was all a very realistic dream. That's why when the news of her nomination for the Awards arrived, she told her brother, "I need to be slapped across my face, *hard*, right now."

Although her brother seemed happy to oblige, it wasn't needed after all—because her mother's warm hug was enough. Her wet cheeks pressed against her own face were enough. Ayaana sighed and realized; *Iyer women are dramatic*.

As soon as she reaches home, she decorates her walls with Raahil's stickers. She notices an unusual neon colored hair tie that immediately makes her smile. *If only I had longer hair...* she thinks. She puts it on her wrist as a bracelet instead. Ayaana even decides to wear it tonight at the party her friends are throwing in honor of her success.

Aside from her musical talents, Ayaana always stands out because of her tattoos. But nobody knows how badly she wants to hide away, to sleep and not wake up, to shut everyone out. She keeps drowning in her mind, wondering whether or not the world would still turn if she was absent. She fantasized about the slow march towards the finish line; she longs for it to be quick. So close to the ending, she can almost touch it.

To hide these true feelings from others, she smiles all the time, but she isn't happy. She is rich, successful and surrounded by friends, but even so, joy is something she doesn't know. It is true what they say; invisible tears have the longest trails.

Getting ready for a party she never wanted, Ayaana practices smiling in front of her mirror. She remembers a time when chords and musical notes were hard lumps stuck in her throat. But, now, she sings, the pain released outside her body, the vibrations of which, she imagines, are felt on a star in a distant galaxy.

After practicing her smile for another five minutes, she books a cab and promises her mother she'll be back before midnight.

Her cab arrives at eight o'clock sharp. She'll make sure to give the driver five stars on the app just for his punctuality. The driver flashes a smile at her as she gets in, and she smiles back. Even from looking at his profile, she can tell he is a handsome, young fellow who looks like he knows it.

A few awkward eye contacts later, Ayaana notices that they are on an unfamiliar route. She pretends to speak on the phone with her brother, loudly describing every turn the driver takes. Ayaana has read crime documentaries about cab drivers who turned out to be serial killers. She smirks on the inside knowing that she's smarter than he is. This is when her brother actually calls.

She fumbles with her phone until it's silent. Seeing her cab driver stifling his laughs in the rear-view mirror, she becomes so embarrassed that if she turns any redder, she'd resemble a tomato.

At last, after what seems like the longest ride, Ayaana reaches the club—still thoroughly embarrassed but unharmed. She gets out of the car, welcoming the embrace of this sweet summer night. Turning around to pay for her ride, she half expects a snarky comment, but the guy surprises her. He does not accept her money and instead, he smiles at her again and says, "You're smart to be cautious. But not everyone in the world is trying to hurt you. Good day ma'am."

His words were alive, hanging in the air, taunting her. And while she stands there contemplating them, with nobody but a few crickets and a lonely owl to debate with, he drives off, soon being long gone.

After a moment, she turns toward the club and makes her way inside. She's still thinking about what happened when she sees her friends are already waiting for her in the VIP lounge. When they spot her, they begin shrieking and waving. *And the nightmare begins*, she sighs…

After shot after shot of vodka, Ayaana starts to loosen up. Despite being terrible at it, she loves to dance and can't keep herself away from the dance floor any longer. Ignoring everyone and everything around her, it is just her, the music, and the dance floor. After a few songs, she is sweaty; her makeup running and her hair a mess. Moreover, wanting a little space, she excuses herself and goes to the restroom to get some air and to fix her face.

When she's done, she examines the rest of herself in the mirror. The stranger staring back at her looks just fine. After all, not all masks wear off that easily.

Ayaana used to scream silently in the mornings, willing herself to get out of bed. She focuses all of her energy into music and nothing else, including her own wellbeing. Talking to Raahil today opened her eyes. If he can smile, so could she. She'd learn to live and love, one moment at a time, a few blinks away from reality.

Suddenly, in the midst of her thoughts, a girl runs into the bathroom, finds the closest stall, and vomits in the toilet. Ayaana notices she is alone, crying, trying to keep her long hair from falling over her face while she pukes. She eyes the door, waiting for one of the girl's friends to come rushing in to help her, but no one does. Ayaana instinctively gives the girl the neon hair tie from her wrist to help her keep her hair out of her face. The girl mutters something that vaguely sounds like a thank you, before throwing up again.

After a few minutes, the girl, presumably intoxicated, is finally done vomiting. She wipes her mouth, flushes the toilet, and stands on wobbly legs.

"Are you alright? Can I get you something?" Ayaana asks.

"No, thank you," the girl replies between sobs.

"Is there someone with you? Should I call a cab?" Ayaana asks, taking a good look at the girl now that she's facing her. She is chubby with pasty skin, and has midnight eyes and Rapunzel-like hair.

"Someone was with me. But, don't worry, I'll call a friend."

"My name is Ayaana Iyer. Let me know if there's something I can do to help."

"Layla Malik. Nice to meet you. Sorry for all the trouble, though. You are too kind."

"If you don't mind, may I ask what happened?" Ayaana knows it isn't any of her business but she cannot resist a good story.

"Love. Love happened," Layla says.

Ayaana gives her a nervous smile. *How predictable*, she thinks.

Without further explanation, Layla leaves the bathroom, taking Ayaana's hair tie with her. Meanwhile, Ayaana continues standing there, tracing a phantom tie on her wrist. She looks in the mirror once again, thinking about that handsome cab driver from earlier. And this time, she doesn't need to practice her smile. In some parallel world, they would meet again, maybe fall in love. She realizes she should've just asked for his number.

14 July 2023
3:00 a.m.
Evelyn

      Evelyn is running. She is tired. Everything is so blurry. She can hear them running after her. Stumbling over violent pebbles, she smells their lust. Yet, dragging her wobbly legs, she runs. In her heart, she knows this is it. This is how she'll die. Her chest might explode any minute now. She fights for breath. The end of her tunnel paves way for the darkest figure; too scary to embrace and too alluring to ignore.

      The pills forced down her throat are kicking in. She hallucinates, crying. Standing with shaky legs, she wants to give up and let the figure take her. Suddenly, there's a blinding light and a loud whistle. She realizes she is standing on a railway track, facing a train coming at her. Unable to move, she closes her eyes, her whole life flashing in front of her. She is as ready as she could be to face what comes next, when someone grabs her by the arm and yanks her off the track. The train passes by and the cold wind slaps her face.

10 June 2022
Aanjaney and Evelyn

Aanjaney and his two best friends are on their way to a movie theatre. He looks outside the window from the front passenger seat, and when his eyes land on someone he doesn't expect, Aanjaney feels the world stop spinning for a few seconds. He sees *her* walking alongside her friends. He cannot breathe or speak.

His friends see her too, saying something that Aanjaney can't hear. His heart is beating fast, and he works to calm it. He finally finds his voice again and asks his friend to turn the car around. He has to see her. He has to listen to her voice and look into those beautiful eyes once again.

His friend complies, and as he makes the U-turn, all of Aanjaney's memories come flooding back. She is a poison his veins would readily welcome. Just thinking about their time together makes his heart heavy and his mind blurry. Her soul stretches deeper than the oceans. He has always been able to see her, beneath the veil of calmness and the stormy front; crashing against the rocks, each drop embodying all of his tear beads, boundless like the horizon that she so badly wanted to kiss. Under the spell of tides, she is like a dream drifting away.

Now, she stands just a few meters away from him, as lovely as ever. He gets out of the car and their eyes lock for a moment. Then, she looks down, breaking eye contact, losing all the color from her face. *She is as pale as a moon flower on July morning,* he thinks.

As the world spins around her, she feels an overwhelming sense of dizziness. Edges of her vision becomes hazy, and her limbs feel like lead. With one step backward, she crumples down, the concrete floor rushing to meet her. She hears distorted noises coming from far away.

Twenty minutes later, in a bleak room filled with a sterilized smell, Aanjaney sits next to her lying body. He inspects every inch of her face, lost in a memory he thought he had long forgotten. Many years ago, on a beautiful, starry night, she stood defenseless before him, as he unhooked her soul. The facade slipped from her shoulders, sliding down her hips, like a flowing brook. He remembers being marveled at the beauty exposed, stripped of doubt and naked, yet wholly clothed. It was the day their souls made love to one another. Right as he begins to feel tears form in his eyes, she wakes up, blinking owlishly at him.

"What happened?" she asks, looking around.

"It was just low blood pressure. You hit your head, though, and had to get a tiny stitch. Here, drink some water," he says, handing her a small, plastic bottle he had gotten from the vending machine.

"Thank you."

"You've changed," he says, his head drooping.

"What do you mean?" she asks, tucking her hair behind her ears.

"Just, *'thank you'*? Really, Evy? You can't even look me in the eye, can you? Do you know how long it took for me to feel normal again? Trying to rip you out of my mind and hurting myself more and more in the process. Your memories are just as stubborn as you, you know," he says with a slight tremble in his lips and a storm in his eyes.

"I don't understand. You were the one who…"

"The Evy I knew wasn't a coward. So, keep your *'thank you's'* to yourself. I don't even know who you are anymore. Take care," he says, interrupting her. He rises, about to leave.

"Wait."

He pauses, turning around to look at the puzzled look on her face.

"Why are you calling me a coward when you were the one afraid to have a future with me? *You* are the coward. *You* gave up on us."

"I gave up? I came to see you, Evy, hoping we could try again. Hoping you would maybe give us another chance. But two years ago, you slapped me with a fucking restraining order. What did you expect, huh? I tried. I really tried. You think it was easy? Learning to live without…" he says, breathing heavily, the lump in his throat making it harder to speak.

"I… I don't understand. I didn't file anything against you. Did you really think that I… You think I gave up on us? Is that why you never came back?" she says, burying her face in her hands, breaking into tears.

He rushes to her side and holds her. "Shhh, shhh. It's okay. It's okay, I've got you. I've got you, Evy," he whispers, kissing her head. "It's okay," he mutters to himself under his breath again.

"We... we were... you know. Us."

"I know," he sighs.

After one hour and multiple tiny, rapid forehead kisses later, they part ways again, unwilling to be pawns in life's cruel game once more. But this time, they've truly changed and only one of them for the better.

Aanjaney leaves the hospital with a brimming heart, hoping Evelyn finds the family she deserves with someone who's worthy of her. He leaves knowing that he will always love her, with a prayer in his heart and a smile on his face. For the first time in his life, he is truly brave.

Whereas, Evelyn is left with a swelling hole in her heart, one that is doomed to get bigger and darker until it will ultimately consume her.

Unlike popular belief, love is not blind. It sees everything. It sees through people, the parts of them they didn't know existed. That can scare them. The thought of someone looking at their bare and vulnerable self is terrifying. But being vulnerable together, fully capable of breaking and being broken, and still diving headfirst into it, is downright heroic.

Therefore, no matter where life takes them and how their stories end, Aanjaney Iyer and Evelyn Charles are and always will be heroes.

12 July 2023
12:30 a.m.
Layla

Layla Malik is a Muslim and a lesbian, who loves sex. These statements, if said together or otherwise, in any situation, whatsoever, are likely to cause several heart failures across the country.

There are infinite ways to be a woman, but society still puts people in boxes. The only gender rule that should exist is that there are no rules. And there should be no pre-existing template on how people should look or dress. For our collective perspectives to evolve, to liberate each other, as a society, we need to be able to have difficult and uncomfortable conversations.

Because this is not the current norm, Layla lives in a perpetual state of fear, of these conversations, of never fitting in, of looking weak. This long list of angst is what drives her. It has become the focal point of her existence, that fear. It is a lonely way to live, but she has learnt to be okay with that. On the other hand, being dumped by the potential love of her life, not so much.

After being dumped over the phone, Layla decided to gain more perspective. So, she went to the club to have a deep life talk with Rum and Coke, but instead of finding the meaning to life there, she ended up throwing up in the bathroom while a stranger stood there, not knowing how to help.

After the club, Layla went home. Her pet, the one living being who has never given her labels, is waiting for her at the door. Snowy, a beautiful Lhasa Apso, looks like a disappointed parent. *Is it the rum, or is Snowy really giving me the "we need to talk" look?* she wonders, but of course, she'll never know.

Layla changes into her most comfortable PJs. She runs her hand through her long, tangled hair and takes a closer glance at the weird-looking hair tie. It makes her smile, thinking about that random act of kindness from a stranger. She pulls her hair into a messy bun with the same tie and decides to stalk her ex on Instagram until her eyes tire out.

Before the break up, this was the first time she had allowed herself to fall in love. Her ex, a gorgeous and theoretically unattainable woman, had, and still has, all the strings to her heart.

Layla loves movies. She loves everything about them. So ever since she was a child, she fantasized about living in one. For most of her life, she was either a villain's daughter or a heroine's friend. Sometimes, she was nothing but a camera lens. Even today, that's what she does. She sees and creates, never once being the main character.

Layla wants something so extraordinary and breathtaking. She wants a well-crafted script that'll keep surprising her. She wants magic and power. But sadly, there's no such thing as a perfect cinema. Or so she thought—until, one fine day, someone walked into her frame and proved her wrong.

The lighting was poor, angles weren't flattering, but right then and there, was the key moment; Layla's key moment. And just like that, everything started to fit. She realized she was not another secondary character. This was *her* story, and she would tell it *her* way. Because now she knows that if she plays her part right, the end will be legendary.

Layla is sure her lover would come back, though. She always does. But this time, when she does, Layla is determined to make her see that she's the one for her.

Layla is deep in thought when the doorbell rings. She gets up and opens the door. It is the ever-magnificent Evelyn Charles, absolutely hammered with a cigarette loosely hanging on her lips. With her long, dark lashes, doe eyes, lustrous black hair, and a drool-worthy body, she has it all.

"Hey babe!" Evelyn says, smiling.

"What are you doing here? You broke up with me. *Over the phone,* remember?"

"That was a dick move. Sorry."

"Sorry is not going to cut it, Evy."

"How many times have I told you, *do not* call me that," Evelyn says with a clenched jaw.

Layla is tense now. She cannot mess it up this time. "You're completely right. I'm sorry. Why don't you come in? Let's talk. Okay?"

Evelyn brushes past her without saying anything and begins walking up the staircase that leads to roof.

"Are you sure that's a good idea, given the condition you're in? Layla asks, and is ignored by Evelyn, again. She decides that if she can't persuade Evelyn to pick a safer talking place, she will at least join her on the roof. Layla sighs, but follows her up the stairs.

They sit there in silence, with city lights below and stars above them. Layla wishes they could stay here forever like this, basking in the moonlight, with nothing but love and peace between them. "Now that I see through your eyes, stars shine a little brighter every night," Layla says, leaning her head on Evelyn's shoulders.

"You could never," Evelyn says emotionless, gazing into nothing. "Imagine a stranger's heart beating in sync with yours at this moment. Breath aligned, someone, someplace, right now."

Layla closes her eyes, aware of her every heartbeat, breathing in and out.

Meanwhile, Evelyn dreams of a particular familiar stranger. She closes her eyes too and imagines his heart beating in sync with hers. His breaths aligning hers. She hears an echo. "Evy..." it says.

"Just keep feeling. Lose yourself in the connection you know nothing of. Imagine your living, breathing human bond. You want to see. You want to know. Strangely, not knowing made you powerfully pregnable. And this moment of realization is peacefully disturbing," Evelyn says, with her eyes still closed and a smile on her face.

"You're amazing. There's nobody like you. Really... It's one of the many things that made me fall for you."

"There's nobody like anybody, Layla. And you're in love with the idea of me. I know you believe it's real. And I am so sorry that I make you sad, but would you prefer I lie to you and give you false hopes about ice-creams and rainbows?" she asks, her words slurring.

"What are you doing here then, Evelyn? Do you even like me?"

Evelyn is silent. She keeps looking at the stars. "Why do stars shine? Do you think they know people wish on them?"

"What?"

"Stars. What makes them shine?"

"Why does it even matter?" Layla asks, growing impatient.

Evelyn leans towards Layla, their bodies pressed together, sending shivers down Layla's spine. They kiss slowly at first. With one hand on her waist, Layla holds Evelyn in place while gently running her fingers through her hair with the other hand.

"Nuclear fusion."

"What?" Evelyn asks out of breath.

"Stars shine because of nuclear fusion."

Evelyn chuckles. "Nerdy and needy. Not bad," she says, before resuming their kiss. She pulls Layla's hair down and puts the hair tie on her own wrist. They hastily tug at each other's clothes, desperate to quench the throbbing ache.

Layla can't sing. Yet, there's a music note somewhere trapped inside her. She can't dance. Yet, her body is synced to a certain rhythm. Evelyn is capable of heightening and dulling her senses. The color of her eyes, the smell of her body, the taste of her lips, the sound of her heartbeat, and the feeling of her touch... *Oh, her touch.*

Electricity courses through Layla's veins with endless sparks of passion. On the other hand, that amazing moment when her senses are dulled, vision blurred, and hearing impaired as they become one. That moment when love triumphs all, when Layla worships every inch of Evelyn's skin, as she writes a poem on her body with her lips; a poem of love, a poem of desire, a poem of a never-dying promise. They lay there on the cold, concrete floor, with nobody but the moon to judge them.

"This was the last time," Evelyn says, standing up and shimmying back into her skinny jeans.

"What do you mean, last time?" Layla asks, getting up as well.

"Much better than a phone call, right?" Evelyn asks, winking.

Layla stands there, suddenly aware of her nakedness. This isn't supposed to happen. They are meant to be together. Layla knows it. This shouldn't be the end. It can't be.

"Why? Why did you come here and have sex with me if you wanted to break my heart again? Why?" Layla asks, fighting for breath.

"Because it feels good. We had a good time, didn't we?" Evelyn says, buttoning her shirt.

"I love you. Please don't do this," Layla begs, feeling a thousand needles pricking her heart.

"I have told you many times, Layla, I'm not looking for love. You knew that from the beginning. We can't continue this loop. You will always want more. And seriously, my eardrums will explode if I hear you whine about 'love' one more time. You should learn to chill. Bring it down a few decibels."

Layla is speechless. Her whole world is tearing apart.

"Also, I'm keeping this hair tie. It will be a nice souvenir. You couldn't pull it off anyway," Evelyn says playfully, completely oblivious to Layla's state of mind.

"It's that agent guy, right? You fucking him? Like you fucked half the city?"

"Woah! Buckle down Mother Teresa. And who? Raphael? Gross! He's like a hundred years old. Layla, pull yourself together, okay? Can you do that for me? You are going to be okay." Evelyn kisses her on the cheek.

Layla pushes her away, but Evelyn grabs her face. Layla refuses to look at her.

"You belong, Layla. There is enough space for everybody to grow. Stop attacking somebody for a little bit of sunshine. We have the sun. Someone else's existence is no threat to you."

"Leave!" Layla screams.

"Have a good life," Evelyn says as she closes the door behind her.

Layla stands there, frozen. Evelyn took all the air in the room and she is left blue, and dying.

15 July 2023
Ayaana

With every breath you inhale, somebody, somewhere takes their first, and with every exhale, somebody, somewhere has taken their last. Life passes us by between these microseconds, so fleeting, yet worth everything.

Ayaana zones in and out through the pitter patter of rain on her windowsill. It is officially monsoon season, and yet another news coverage on Evelyn's tragedy is playing on her TV. The rain drops are hitting the roof so loudly that she has to turn the volume on the TV up. A few minutes later, she tosses the remote away and grabs her phone. Ayaana chews the inside of her cheeks, while scrolling through the fifteen messages she left for her brother. He hasn't been home since he found out.

Seeing Evelyn's face on the news again, Ayaana's mind travels to another stormy day, years ago, when she wrote her first song, "Rain." It was inspired by a conversation between her brother and his then girlfriend, Evelyn Charles. The three of them were eating pizza and watching TV when Evelyn suddenly looked at Aanjaney and told him that he was like the smell of first rain to her. As cliché as that was, it became Ayaana's inspiration for her debut song.

Later that night, her brother called her into his room. "Listen, I need a favor," he said.

"Three conditions," she responded, smiling from ear to ear.

"Ugh. Okay, fine," he said, rolling his eyes.

"Ice cream. Double chocolate chip."

"Done."

"Full control of the TV remote for a week."

"I hate you so much right now."

"There's more."

"Yes, your highness," he said, sarcasm dripping from each word.

"I am getting a tattoo, and you can't get mad."

"What?!"

"*Please…?*" she asked with puppy eyes.

"I'll think about that. I'll have to see what you choose before I decide whether I'll be mad or not. And now, about the favor…" He showed her a shimmering, silver bracelet with iridescent beads that mimicked the colors of the Milky Way, with charms of stars dangling on a delicate chain. "It's for Evelyn's birthday. I had it custom made. You are a girl, right? I mean, sort of... So, tell me, will she like it?"

"First of all, *'sort of'*?" she asked, pretending to be hurt.

"Alright, alright. Now, tell me."

"It's beautiful. But what does it mean? The whole galaxy theme?"

"It means we'll always find each other under the stars. I know it sounds lame, but Evy and I promised that to each other when we were stargazing on the high school football field."

"You both are so adorable that I want to throw up in your face. She'll love it. Don't worry."

The doorbell rings, breaking Ayaana's trance. She switches off the TV, pushes the intrusive, overlapping commentary inside her head away, and opens the door to a handsome, dirty boy with missing teeth.

12 July 2023
Raahil

When a story is born, the writer becomes the God of tiny and convoluted dimensions. In Raahil's story, there are human ant colonies and shiny, leather shoes stomping on them. There are raindrops falling off asbestos sheets and rainbows bouncing off dumpsters. And in between all of this, there are incorruptible hearts full of love and joy.

Raahil eagerly awaits his music lessons with Ayaana. It is all he can talk about, much to the annoyance of his beloved Amina. Now, to help pass the time, they race on muddy roads, trying to outrun the old bicycle tires they roll down the road with sticks, a fun game that is off-limits to children with nice shoes and real toys. But them, they are free to run around as they please—not caring about global warming or who's going to win the next election or what celebrity is getting married that week.

No one is stopping them from laughing so hard that they need to take a break in order to catch their breath. A few seconds later, they look at each other and burst into another fit. Little moments like these create pure happiness for them, untainted by the smell of fresh printed currency. Memories like these ones will be forever etched in their hearts. Whether they realize it or not, Raahil and Amina are luckier than most.

Laughing, running, chasing, and panting they reach Amina's home.

"No matter what you say, Zaydan Bhai is the best. Did you know he bought me a full plate of biriyani yesterday?" Raahil says, parking the tires on the steps leading up to the quaint house.

"Raahil, you tube light," Amina says, shaking her head.

"Ay, don't call me stupid, you… you mosquito," he says, sticking his tongue out.

"I maybe tiny but definitely not dumb enough to give a 2000 rupee note for a biriyani and be happy about it."

"It doesn't matter. He is powerful, and I want to be like him when I grow up."

"I want to be an athlete," she says dreamily.

"What's an athlete?" Raahil asks, scrunching his nose.

"It's someone who can run real fast. Sharada Auntie told me all about it. If a runner is good enough, they are given good things, you know, like money. And with enough money, they'll become famous. I want to be famous everywhere. And tall. And… and very pretty," she rambles.

"Who's stupid now?"

Amina smacks Raahil on his head. They hear somebody loudly clear their throat. They look behind them and see Amina's father standing in the doorway.

"Don't tease my daughter, son. She'll be the one bailing you out of jail someday if you keep working for that Zaydan."

"Abbu!" Amina runs to hug her father, and he kisses her forehead.

Raahil stands up and looks at him. He sees Amina's father has bloodshot eyes and can smell his stench from where he stands. It's the same smell most men in their colony have, especially at nights. It's the kind of smell that scares both Raahil and Amina because something bad always happens. Always.

"Amina, my angel, aren't you forgetting something?"

"No, Abbu," Amina sighs, fetching crumpled rupees from under her pillow.

"Good girl. Is that all, dear?"

"Yes, Abbu."

"Tomorrow, I'll take you to the carousel. Promise.

Amina smiles while Raahil silently watches with pursed lips.

"Now, let's go get some ice gola."

"Seriously?"

"Haan, seriously," he says, ruffling her hair.

"Yay!" She starts jumping around.

"Raahil, come with us. This girl won't go two steps without you to make fun of."

Raahil can't help but smile, seeing his best friend tugging her father's kurta, looking at him with her big, dragonfly eyes.

"Did you know your nose flares up when you smile like that? It makes you look like a baby pig."

"Shut up."

Raahil and Amina walk on the pavement, hand in hand, counting streetlights as they go. After a quick ten minutes, they arrive at their destination.

As Amina's father buys the golas, Raahil and Amina hop on zebra crossing, pretending to be keys on a piano. After a couple of minutes, her father walks towards them, carefully holding three ice golas in his hands, when suddenly, they see a car skid out of control; its bright headlights obscuring everything except the fear flashing in her father's face as he drops the golas. He begins to run towards the children but doesn't reach them.

Loud sirens that replace the screams leave behind one word reverberating in stagnant air, "Abbu." Whereas smell of diesel and smoke, followed by that of blood, leave behind a tiny trace of tobacco and liquor, making the scene smell of home.

This blurry life-altering second will live forever in cold, sweaty nightmares, lurking behind every smile and tear. Such a funny word, forever.

12 July 2023
Evelyn

We have been indoctrinated to fear things that might set us free. Evelyn spent a lot of time trying to understand what's wrong with the world and why certain things happen when they shouldn't. Why did her existence cause her trauma? Why are some people set to fail in this world? Why is it that people don't see that everybody loses against patriarchy? Why aren't people more terrified of climate change? She discovers trying to find logic is unproductive and exhausting.

We live in a collection of a million worlds entangled into a beautiful mess. The universe, as we see it, is different for every single person. For instance, A, B, and C are walking through a park. A sees a beautiful girl smile at him. B sees a dozen wild flowers. Whereas, C looks despairingly at his worn-out shoes. His world. Her world. My world. Your world. It's all the same, yet entirely different. It's nothing but another one of God's oxymorons laughing at us. Some people spend their entire life waiting for an epiphany. While some live.

Evelyn Charles belonged to the latter. With every feather shed in the wind and any path of sand she grazed; she used it to soar higher.

But now, she is in her room, absently playing with a hair tie she took from Layla last night, staring at the dark, wood-paneled walls and recapping her life until this moment. Amidst all the chaos, Evelyn made a home in a world entirely of her own making. An orphan girl turned actress. Begging for chances, saving up for auditions, and making uncountable sacrifices, she became an incorrigible presence in the industry. She beat the odds. Evelyn is a dreamer who could never relate to anyone, or reality for that matter.

But she is quite okay with not making sense, with being an unsolvable mystery. She speaks a language nobody can decipher. Nobody but *him*, whom she lost. She remembers it like yesterday, the day they met.

She was fifteen, sitting in biology class, tuning the noise out and zeroing in on birds chirping outside. The distraction did not last long, though. Soon, the birds flew away and she found herself back in the room. Hearing girls whispering and giggling, she looked up to see what the sudden commotion was about and found the tall, handsome object of their interest; a new kid walking through the door. She noticed the slight slant to his shoulders and the way he ran his fingers through his hair, a nervous habit she figured.

He smiled in her direction, but his smile was something different than she had ever seen. It made Evelyn's heart feel warmer than it had ever been.

Luckily, there was always an empty seat next to her since nobody liked sitting next to the 'weird' girl. *As fate would have it, the seat was never to be empty again.* Close up, she noticed he had sad eyes, which strangely, she immediately adored.

"Hey, Linda. Glad I found you. This place is so confusing."

Evelyn thought to herself, *Who the hell's Linda?* But out loud, she said while blushing, "Yeah, thank God you did."

"When my mum said I had a distant cousin in this school, I had no idea she meant we would be sharing a class."

Evelyn smiled, nodded affirmatively, and played along. She kept up this pretense for an hour.

They talked and laughed, something new for them both. He thought it was bonding with a distant family member. She thought it was magic.

Punctuating the moment, a girl walked towards them, her shirt too tight and skirt too high. "I heard you were looking for me. I'm Linda," she said, batting her eyelashes.

Evelyn sat there, hoping he wouldn't humiliate her in front of Barbie.

Surprising them both, he said, "You heard wrong. Sorry."

As soon as she left, Evelyn buried her face in her hands.

"Hey, it's okay. If it makes you feel any better, I had figured it out already, anyways."

"What? When?!"

"In about the first five seconds of us talking," he said, smiling.

"Oh, God! Just kill me now," she said. He laughed in his infectiously beautiful way.

"Let's start again. Shall we?"
Evelyn nodded sheepishly. Holding out his hand, he said,

"I'm Aanjaney Iyer."
She looked at his enticing glum eyes and said,

"Evelyn."

"I'm gonna call you Evy, alright?" he asked, making her smile in response.

"If you knew I was lying, why didn't you say something? Why did you go along with it?" she asked.

"Why did you smile back at me?" he asked in response.

"I couldn't help it."

"Me neither."

That was the beginning of the rest of their lives, a beginning to forever. Or so they had hoped.

They swam so far, only to drown at the shallow end. Years later, bottling up her pain, Evelyn let it kill her. Inhaling truth, she was reduced to ash. Before she knew it, she became an addict. Loss does strange things to people. There is a huge void in her heart that keeps getting bigger and darker. She yearned for a breeze that'd take her to him. In her dreams, they land somewhere together. Just him and her.

However, Evelyn kept filling the hole with drugs and sex. But even after the effects came to an end, the hole was still there. So, she did it again. And again. All for a fleeting, temporary pain-free moment.

After a year of self-destruction, Evelyn is finally in better shape now. Coming back from her rock bottom was nearly impossible. She owes it to her agent, Raphael Adler, for pulling her out before it was too late. But her career and public image are beyond repair. Nobody wants to sign her anymore. On the brink of depression, she made a decision, which in hindsight, might be the stupidest thing she's ever done: Layla Malik.

In the beginning, Layla was just another distraction for her. Although, she'd made sure that Layla knew it for what it was and nothing more, it didn't work out as she had hoped. Evelyn likes to think that this breakup will be a turning point in Layla's life for she'll finally start putting herself first. The only thing that Evelyn regrets is dragging their friendship through the mud. She needs to apologize for being inconsiderate and making Layla feel used.

Ending their relationship was the right call to make, but the way she did it was selfish. She personally knows what heartache feels like and wouldn't wish it on anybody. Evelyn only realizes all this now that the alcohol is out of her system.

Evelyn looks at the neon hair tie once again and knows what must be done. With a determined look on her face, she walks out the door. That's when she sees, walking by her perfectly manicured lawn, a really pissed-off Raphael, carrying what looks like a tabloid in his right hand.

"Hey Raph! What's up, old man?"

Raphael Adler is a forty-eight-year-old, short man with salt and pepper tousled hair, three ex-wives, two blocked arteries, and a protruding belly. Waving the tabloid upon seeing Evelyn, he says through clenched teeth and fists, "You and I are going to have a talk. Let's go for a drive."

Raphael is the closest thing Evelyn has to a family, but she is also aware of his frightening temper. They silently drive for about ten minutes before she can't help herself any longer. "What's the matter?" she asks nervously.

He tosses the tabloid at her that he had been holding earlier and starts yelling. "What is wrong with you?! First, you sabotage your career over some boy and become an addict. Now, *this*. My job isn't cleaning up your mess, princess."

Evelyn looks at the tabloid and sees an intimate picture of Layla and her. Layla looks so happy in it. Evelyn smiles at the picture. "They didn't get my good side," she says.

"Is everything a joke to you?"

"It's just a sleazy magazine. People will forget about all of this soon. Don't worry," she says, shrugging.

"Your career is in jeopardy. In no time, you'll be out of a job."

"Thanks for the motivation. Really appreciate it," Evelyn says, rolling her eyes.

"Do not roll your eyes at me, young lady. I'm serious. You can't just—"

"*Young lady?* Really?! Who says that anymore? Man, you're old!"

"You just—"

"I broke it off, Raph. Last night. But I behaved like an entitled, straight white man, *ugh*." The thought disgusts her. "Let me just go over there and see her."

"No."

"What?"

"I said, *no*. You can't be seen anywhere near her. Plus, you'll only be making things harder for her. Let her be."

Evelyn hates being told what to do. But on the other hand, maybe Raph's right. Maybe she should just leave Layla alone, giving her the space and time to move on peacefully. Evelyn hands him the neon hair tie and says, "Then, do me a favor at least. Give this to her. Tell her I'm sorry for everything."

"I don't see why that's necessary," Raphael says.

"I wasn't asking," Evelyn says, on the verge of losing her cool.

"Hmm." His jaw tightens, his knuckles turn white on the steering wheel.

"I don't tolerate being talked to like a child, Raphael. You're not my dad," she says, pushing him further over the edge.

Blinded by fury, he finally snaps. "That's right! I'm *not* your father. And thank God for that," he spits, speeding faster and faster with every word.

"Raph, please slow down," Evelyn begs with wet eyes and shaky hands, torn between her past, present, and a dubious future.

And just as fast as he was pushed over the edge, was he able to bring himself back to solid ground. "I… I didn't mean that. I don't know why

I..." He takes his eyes off the road to meet her tear-stained gaze.

Evelyn looks ahead and screams, seeing two children playing on the road. She grabs the wheel, forcing the car to take a sharp, right turn. It was too late before Raphael hit the brakes.

In that one second, as their faces pale and bodies freeze in fear, they hear only one word, "Abbu!"

13 July 2023
Ayaana

After swimming in the turquoise sea, Ayaana walks on red sands. She spots an ice-cream vendor dressed in black and he smiles at her. She smiles back, searching her pocket for coins, and finds one silver needle. He gives her a vanilla ice-cream in exchange for her needle, which glistens in the sun before melting into her palm. And now, she's holding a sword with a white blade.

Ayaana hears a child's laugh from afar. She sees a woman pointing at beautiful, white buildings in a line. She follows the laugh and runs, entering the last building. Suddenly, it's getting hot in there. It's scorching. She sees red and orange and blue. Fire swallows the building. And now, it's gone. There's silence. No laughs or cries. The white walls are gray now. But still as clean as before.

She stands still and dares not move. To her horror, the building reappears and starts rolling like a ball on the ground. Windows become doors. She leaps and bounces through them. The walls are cold as she runs on them. The building is standing again. She hears nothing but the screams of silence. She knows silence isn't good. Cold isn't either. The building beast is ominously still, as if savoring its last moment. She wonders what happens next.

Ayaana takes small steps to the window. Fear consumes her as she sees more buildings fall. The first one falls on the second. The second on the third. She witnesses a domino effect. It's fast and approaching. She screams till her lungs hurt, but no voice comes out. A turquoise tsunami washes over her. She is wet but unhurt.

She opens her eyes and sees her mother chiding her, "What kind of lady sleeps till noon? How will you ever get married?"

She rubs her eyes and thinks, *my walls are so boring.* As soon as she realizes what day it is, she starts panicking. "Why didn't you wake me up sooner, Amma? Raahil will be here any minute now. I can't believe I overslept again." She hears her brother scoffing in the adjacent room. "Don't you have a parking ticket to give out?" she yells.

"Shhh, be nice. He's on sick leave," her mother says.

"You know I'm an inspector now, right?" he says, entering her room.

"Ayaana, get ready for breakfast. And Aanjaney, don't piss her off," their mother warns, before leaving the room.

"Ugh, your breath can ward off an anteater," he says to Ayaana, throwing a towel at her face and getting comfortable on her bed.

"Ammaaaaa! He's hurting me," she screams, sticking out her tongue at him.

"Shhh! *Liar*."

"Now, get off my bed, idiot."

"At least I'm not an unplanned child," he says as he looks down, feigning innocence.

"You know I'm not ten. That's not going to work anymore."

"Speaking of ten, what's the deal with that slum boy?"

"His name is Raahil, and he's actually really great."

"You met him like two times. These kids are criminals, Ayaana, or will be."

"That's your uniform talking. You'll love him. I am sure. Now, get out. I need to shower."

"Well, whoever he is, if he's the reason for that smile on your face, that's enough for me."

"What are you talking about? I smile all the time," she says, walking him to the door.

Aanjaneya looks at her in the way only he does. In that moment, she remembers how well they know each other.

"Now, hurry before I finish your food as well."

"You wouldn't dare," Ayaana says, eyeing him, almost as if challenging him.

"Uh-huh, try me."

After a long time, Ayaana is excited about something. The thought of Raahil warms her. In this world, where everything that matters is eventually and irrevocably labeled as a sad cliché, she is on a quest to find true happiness. And the key to happiness, she believes, will be forged by Raahil. She will mentor him and charge gaiety in return.

Ayaana looks at her wrinkly fingers and realizes she's been in the shower for too long. She puts on her clothes and runs down the stairs, joining her family for breakfast.

"Raahil isn't here yet?" she asks.

"Nope, I guess that's how quickly he forgot about you. Which, I don't blame him." He responds with a rascally smile that earns an eye roll from Ayaana.

Their mouths water looking at the dosas and chutneys their mother placed on the dining table. They were about to attack their food when they noticed Amma's face.

"What happened, Amma?" Aanjaney asks, his face etched with concern.

"Where is he? He is supposed to be here. I made his favorite breakfast. Do you think he forgot what day it is?" she says with trembling hands and a puckered forehead.

Ayaana and Aanjaney glance at each other in worry. Their mother has never been the same since their father left. They are aware of her delusions, and to calm the situation, they normally just go along with it. But her paranoia is escalating with every passing day.

"Amma, listen to me—"

Before Ayaana could burst their mother's delusionary world, Aanjaney places his hand on Amma's, and interrupts Ayaana by saying, "Why don't you tell us what day it is. Right, Ayaana?" He looks at her, hoping she will read his face. He breaks a dosa, dips it in chutney, and starts feeding his Amma, who resists it at first.

"You love eating out of my hand. Don't deny it," he says, smiling.

Their mother becomes visibly calmer. In between bites, she begins narrating a tale. Ayaana leans forward, pretending to listen intently to a story they have all heard innumerable times before, each time hoping it would be the last. Aanjaney and Ayaana are forever bonded by the ink that the protagonist of their mother's story left on their skins. They'd wash and wash and wash, yet never be free of it. They will never be free of their father.

Two hours later, the doorbell rings whilst Aanjaney tucks their mother into bed. Ayaana opens the door and finds Raahil smiling at her, flashing those adorable gaps from his missing teeth.

As they make their way into the house, Aanjaney comes out of the back bedroom and meets them near the front door. Ayaana introduces Raahil to her brother, who invites him to the living room. After making sure everyone is well acquainted, Ayaana excuses herself and goes to her room, leaving a man and a boy smiling awkwardly at each other. After a few moments, she returns with a guitar in her hand and sees the two getting along like kindergarteners. What happened in the few minutes that she was gone will always be a mystery.

"You said you'd come in the morning. What happened?" she asks Raahil.

"Oh, that! There was a funeral I had to go to, no big deal," he replies.

"Whose?" asks Aanjaney, baffled.

"My best friend's father," he says to Aanjaney. Then, turning to Ayaana, "Remember Amina? I told you about her. Yeah, her Abbu died last night. Car accident."

The Iyer siblings look at each other, shocked at the impassive tone an eight-year-old boy used to talk about death.

13 July 2023
Raphael

Raphael was eight years old when his uncle first came for him. He knew it was wrong and wanted to burst into tears, and upon seeing Raphael's emotional state of being, his uncle had said, "Shhh, boys don't cry."

After surviving his uncle, Raphael had watched his father abuse his mother for years until one day, he had had enough and fought back for her. Even with a bloody lip and bruised form, there was neither a snivel nor a tear. Because he had learned from a young age that *boys don't cry.* Nobody would ever know the reason for his compulsive neatness or the consistent red marks on his body. There would be no #metoo moment for him because his armor was designed from the fear Raphael induced in others now, a fact that his failed marriages corroborate.

Raphael hears that little girl's voice over and over all night. He can't sleep. The air is unusually cold in his room. He hugs his blanket tight. He then lets go in order to cover his ears using both of his hands, but the screams don't seem to stop. The little girl's voice contained the worst kind of pain; the kind which the physical body is unaware of. It is the saddest thing Raphael has ever heard. He can feel the despair on his skin somehow. That's another stain on his already dirty skin. That little girl's screams were like intense violin notes, and he felt the strings vibrate, almost as clearly as he felt the car smashing into the gola stand.

Evelyn had left him a message after the incident, asking him to get more information on that little girl and to find out whether she had any remaining family members. If she didn't, Evelyn wanted him to then look into the adoption procedure. He can picture Evelyn pacing the halls all night, talking out loud to herself before deciding she wanted to adopt the little girl.

He isn't sure if it was his remorse that drove him to act on it so quickly, or his genuine interest in the little girl's well-being, but he immediately talked to the Child Protection Services about Amina, as Evelyn asked. He found out that the little girl did not have any surrounding family members and, surprisingly, because of the situation and Evelyn's influence, the adoption procedures were flexible.

Raphael's muscles tense just thinking about the alternate life Amina would have had if not for Evelyn, all the horrors she would have been put through. He would've been the reason for all of it. Maybe he should be feared after all… All these years trying to do what's best for Evelyn, now he knows, even *she* isn't safe with him. She never was. He just isn't himself when he's angry. Every time he closes his eyes, Evelyn's frightened face comes to his mind. And the fact that she felt so scared because of him breaks his old heart.

Raphael looks at the clock on the wall and sighs. He knows he's going to need to leave for Evelyn's place soon. There is nothing he can do to run from the screams that will not leave his mind, anyways. He throws his blanket off him and within a minute, he has his shoes on and is leaving the house.

He reaches Evelyn's place at the time she proposed they'd go get Amina. After he knocks on her door, and she opens it to let him in, he notices Evelyn flinch when he hugs her. She says so much without having to speak at all. Both understand everything has changed between them, now that the silence is too damn loud. He gestures to his car that's waiting in the driveway through the still opened door, and without a word, Evelyn passes him and climbs into the passenger seat. He shuts the front door for her and joins her in the car, pulling onto the street to head to Amina's.

The slum Amina lives in makes Raphael want to throw up. He puts a white handkerchief on his face, covering his nose, and makes sure not to touch anything. Meanwhile, Evelyn talks to Amina, telling her all about the castle they will live in and the games they will play. Amina stays quiet, a blank expression on her tired face.

Just when they are about to leave, Amina looks up at them and asks if they can bring Raahil along too. Raphael sees the contorted expression on Evelyn's face before he lies and says, "Why not? Of course, we can bring your friend. I'll make the arrangements. Now, you go with Didi, okay?"

Raphael loads all of Amina's little belongings in the trunk and then opens the door for them. Evelyn and Amina climb into the backseat, and he feels Amina's gaze on their house, assuming she knows it is the last time she will ever see it. That's when he sees a boy further down the street running towards them. At once, Raphael gets in the driver's seat and starts the car. As its engine sings, they drive

away in its claustrophobic succor. In the rear-view mirror, along with whirls of dust and smoke, is a shabby, little slum boy staring.

If you don't stop and look closely at life, you'll end up having blurred memories; something Evelyn told Raphael long ago. Everything that came out of her mouth was like a sharp knife piercing his boxed-up emotions. He hates the fact that he loves her for it. Although, he is just too proud to accept it. She was the one who never feared him no matter what people said, the one who wasn't afraid to call out the misogynist in him, the one who made him want to be better. She is the sun in his life, and he is the black hole that will devour her shine.

After a silent twenty-minute drive, Raphael pulls into her driveway. He grabs the bag from the trunk and hands it to Evelyn. He sees many emotions painting her softened eyes as she looks at Amina. Raphael fiddles with his car keys and then turns around, about to leave, when Evelyn takes his hand and says, "I'm finally going to have a family, Raph. I am finally going to have a home."

Raphael smiles, thinking maybe not everything has changed. But he is surer than ever about the monster that lives in him. His eyes well up,

but he fights it because he knows as well as everyone does, *boys don't cry.*

13 July 2023
Layla

Love is a game, played neither to win nor to lose, but to make people feel a little bit less lonely than usual. We are snowflakes, unique, all of us, melting into something unrecognizable.

Layla was so in love with the idea of love that she betrayed herself. With every second spent wallowing in pity, she was digging her grave. But for now, she wouldn't be the one falling in it.

Layla spends her day in the corner of her dark room, beneath a book shelf. She once believed that between the pages of a book was the loveliest of all places. Now, the same books witness her spiraling in emotions anew. There is food untouched on the table and liquor bottles and cigarette butts lying around, meanwhile she sits in that corner, hair unkempt and eyes burning.

Someone switches on the lights and she grimaces in discomfort. An opaque figure stands in front of her, shielding her from the sudden brightness, making it easier for her to open her eyes. Before her is Evelyn's manager, Raphael Adler, who is scrunching his nose, looking around at her dirty room. "What are you doing here?" she asks, sighing.

"I am here to deliver a message on Evelyn's behalf."

"What do you mean? Speak clearly," she says, getting up.

"Her message is that she doesn't want anything to do with you anymore. So don't bother showing your face around her," he says, rubbing his nose while his eyes dart across the room.

"I don't believe you."

"And I don't care. Evelyn is going to have a fresh start in her life. If you really loved her…"

"Oh, please. Enough with the dramatics, Raphael. You have made your opinions pretty clear before. You called our relationship 'a phase' for God's sake. Leave. *Now*," she says, throwing a book in his direction.

He dodges it and the book hits a wall behind him. "Gladly. I don't want to spend another second with a freak like you." Raphael notices her face tilt, and if her eerie body language frightened him, he would never show it.

"I love her, Raphael. And I know that you are lying because I know Evelyn loves me too. And I will have her."

"Love," he scoffs. "Love is an overrated, overused word. Especially by entitled millennials like you."

"You know what, just stop. Cut the bullshit. Stop pretending to know anything about me or love. Who the fuck gives you the right to decide who I should or shouldn't be with? I represent choice and freedom, and that scares the hell out of privileged little shits like you. Let me tell you this; one day, you'll know what love is. I hope to God that you do. Because I can't even begin to explain it. If I could, I wouldn't be at such a loss for words. How do you expect me to explain the moment my tears meet my smile when I see her? Or about the fireworks in every cell of my being when I'm with her? Or the heart wrenching pain of goodbyes? How do I tell you that my mind chants her name whenever I am lonely? So, I pray to God that you feel it someday too. Then, you'll know. Then, you would be at a loss of words too. And I'll know that you've known."

Raphael has a deadpan expression on his face. He tosses a neon hair tie at her and says, "I think the message is clear."

Layla looks at the hair tie, frozen in place. Meanwhile, Raphael leaves, hoping nothing comes between Evelyn and her happiness any longer.

An hour after Raphael leaves, Layla tears through her destroyed bedroom, looking for her phone. After locating it, she scrolls through her contacts, finding one she had once hoped to never use.

"Zaydan?" she asks when someone answers, fuming with blind rage.

"Yes? Who's this?"

"Layla Malik. It's time for you to start paying up on that debt."

"Uh. Haan, Madam. Anything."

"I want you to kill somebody," she says, crushing the hair tie in her palm, effortlessly subjecting someone to an end so cruel the devil should weep.

15 July 2023
Aanjaney

"The language I use to talk to myself about you will determine how I perceive your memories. Will my brain shut down in fear of agony, or cherish it for the beauty that came with it? My love for you is not conditional on you loving me back or breathing. You exist, that's enough for me, my Evy. It doesn't matter if I never see you again or hear you make that *mhmm* sound when we hug. All that matters is you, now. Always, you. My beautiful Evy. It wasn't enough time. God, I hate time. Before we know it, fall colors will be here, without you. How dare time pass, without you. All the big moments in life, all the Christmases and full moons, without you.

"I hate clocks. Every damn one, each tick, a betrayal. I hate that it won't turn back for you. Truth is, I don't want to move on. I don't want to stop feeling you on my skin. I am, because you were. You saved me. It's painful knowing that you aren't beside me right now, but I will carry you within me, always. I am sorry. I love you so, so much," saying this aloud, Aanjaney Iyer, drops to his knees, breaking into tears on Evelyn's grave.

It starts to rain. He chuckles, wiping his tears, thinking about Evelyn's love for a dramatic scene. She would've loved it. Raindrops cling to his eyelashes and to the tip of his nose, each drop kissing away a little bit of pain. He looks up and smiles, knowing there's only one person capable of doing this to him.

He is taken by surprise as the black clouds are suddenly replaced by the inside of an umbrella. Holding the shaft, there's an old man gesturing for him to get up. He recognizes him as Raphael.

They walk to a shaded spot, and after closing his umbrella, Raphael says, "Yesterday was the will reading."

"Hmm. I don't know what that has to do with me."

"You are right; it doesn't. All her money will be untouched until her ward, Amina is eighteen."

"Her what?"

Aanjaney listens as Raphael fills him in on everything that happened in the span of that life-altering week. "So… she brought Amina home right before she… um…"

"Died. She died, Raphael." The two men stand there, in uncomfortable silence, mourning a woman they adored but failed to protect.

"There was a letter. She wrote letters for people to read after she's gone."

"That sounds like something she would do."

Without any more of an explanation, Raphael hands Aanjaney the letter and is about to leave when he stops him.

"That restraining order; it was you, wasn't it?"

"Did she know?" he asks, his lips set in a grim line.

"Deep down, she knew, but I don't think she wanted to believe it was you who broke her dreams."

"I did it for her. It was all for her own good. Her future. I loved her…" he explains exasperatedly.

"And what good did that do her?" Aanjaney asks, looking up at the clouds, with a distant look on his face.

Raphael walks away without saying a word.

Now that Aanjaney is alone once more, he carefully opens the envelope, seeing it's a little wet from the rain, and pulls out the letter. He carefully holds the piece of paper and starts reading.

Hi there,

So, yeah. I'm dead. Are you crying?

It's two in the morning. My room is filled with the smell of freshly-bloomed jasmines from outside, but they're not half as pretty as you, I swear. Many years ago, do you know what I told people when they asked me how we were so in love all the time? I told them it's because we count stars at night together and give shapes to clouds during the day. Now, I don't know where you are or how you are doing. But I do know that you are still somewhere under those few billion stars we counted. After you were gone, I remember missing you between my laughs and all the imaginary kisses we shared. You and I, we made a pretty great team—all the weirdness included.

All the secrets beyond the skies, layers and layers of history safeguarded by the earth, and the never-ending horizon. Yet, it's strange how two tiny specks find each other, unlocking magic as limitless as the cosmos. It's fascinating that mere fragments of this marvelous oeuvre have a unique story written for them in the stars. Sadly, our story reached an expiry date. But that doesn't make it any less real. The point is, I want you to live your life. I am glad I met you, Aanjaney Iyer. Now, whatever happens next, I know I have lived because I have loved.

Eventually, the dusk of your life will open its sleepy eyes, ready to show you the incredible morning. When the first rays come knocking on your windows, don't be afraid to pull up the blinds. You'll see. You'll see that light won't hurt. I don't know when or how I might die. I just hope it's not too soon. I used to think of time as sand slipping away from my feet. When we were together, those sands held my roots. We grew up laughing, loving, and making mistakes together with a fortunate stroke of serendipity. Now, I am not so sure... I just... Did I find a family, Aanjaney? Did I die sad? I am sure Raphael will take care of everything. He wouldn't let me die like an old maiden. Beneath all that anger, he is a sweet, little man. Old, but still sexy, right?

Don't miss me too much, okay? Now, stop worrying.

I liked you because I thought you were perfect. I loved you when I realized you weren't. There's magic in errors, darling. Real stuff.

So, be happy. Love hard. Be fierce.

Yours,
Yours

(PS: Get ready for some serious haunting.)

Aanjaney folds the letter neatly before putting it in his pocket. He walks into the rain for one final touch.

15 July 2023
Ayaana and Raahil

"Chai or bournvita?" Ayaana asks Raahil.

"Coffee."

"Nope. Bournvita it is."

"Okay," he says, shrugging.

"Now, practice those chords I taught you," she instructs, handing him her guitar. Heading towards the kitchen, she notices an ugly bag, the color of wet mud, on the couch beside Raahil. It looks like it has been dragged through dirt and gravel.

"What's in that? Why do you always carry it around?" she asks, picking it up.

"*Don't!*" he yells at her, snatching it out of her hands. Contents from the bag fall on the floor. "Look what you did. These are my things. Mine," he says, promptly scooping everything up.

"Wait." She picks up a distinguishable silver bracelet. "Where did you get this?" Ayaana asks in a tight, brittle voice.

"I... It's mine," Raahil says.

Aanjaney walks into the living room, wet from head to toe. Ayaana swiftly puts the bracelet out of his sight behind her back. It digs into her palm as she nervously tightens her grip. "What were you doing in the rain? Where did you go without telling anybody?" she asks him.

He ignores her question and eyes her suspiciously, looking at Raahil and then back at her. "You are doing that thing with your face," he says finally.

"What thing?" Ayaana asks.

"You are clearly hiding something. What's in your hand?" he asks, grabbing her hand by force and finding the bracelet in it.

Aanjaney and Ayaana exchange a look, a wordless conversation before she turns her gaze towards Raahil. A few seconds later, Aanjaney grabs Raahil by his collar and presses him into a wall.

"Start. Explaining. Right. Now," Aanajney threatens.

Ayaana notices a vein throbbing in her brother's forehead as he slams his fist on the table. She tries to speak but finds herself incapable of forming coherent sentences. Raahil, on the other hand, with his head held high and steady gaze, looks like he is daring the policeman to do his worst.

"Okay, okay. I'll tell you everything," Raahil eventually says.

14 July 2023
3:00 a.m.
Raahil

Raahil likes the quietness of night and the sound of crickets. It's the only time he is truly himself. There are no shadows towering over him or the need for fake, wide smiles. He carries a plastic bag and collects garbage along the way. He gets paid two rupees for every bag full of trash, and this is the only time of the day without any competition.

There's a railway track between the woods and his colony, a few meters away from Zaydan Bhai's place. He sees a woman running on the track, her hair strewn all over her face, her arms flailing around in a dead manner, and her knees scraped. She is crying. Raahil runs towards her. Suddenly, there's a whistle. He hears a train approaching, louder with every passing second. He runs faster.

Reaching her, he grabs her hand and yanks her away. The train passes by, missing them by inches, the gust of wind making their hair and clothes dance, as its light falls on her pale, tired face. Now, there's darkness once again, demanding a tight embrace.

They hear voices of men from afar. Raahil takes her to the woods and gestures to her to be quiet. She stands behind him as he monitors the area. He turns back to tell her that the men left but only the trees hear him. She is nowhere to be found. On the ground, between the twigs, something silver shines.

14 July 2019
Layla

In the heart of every oppressor, there is a gap where self-love should be. And in that gap, fear lives. Hate is the only emotion that comes closest to defining love. It's funny how two emotions that are completely opposite can be so strikingly parallel. Presence of one openly defies the other. Yet, both are somehow symbiotically existential in human minds. They are extreme, powerful, and domineering in their own dimensions.

Layla Malik, not so long ago, dived into a sea of passion. It was an instinct, a wonderful moment of madness. But she started sinking. Even though she believed that there was no better way to die than to drown in one's love, one question remained. Would Evelyn let her hit rock bottom, or swim with her until oblivion? As soon as Layla found the answer, another madness replaced the existing one.

Mr. Malik, her father, was a homophobe, so Layla seldom had any contact with him. Last year, he died of obviously unnatural causes, making Layla the sole heir of all his money and the reputation that preceded their family name. She built her success on those blood-stained currencies.

Zaydan is a local mercenary who owed a lot of money to her father, the Corleone to every scumbag like him. She knows Zaydan and all about his child trafficking business. He disgusts her. But she disgusts herself even more, going back to the very thing she ran away from.

"How'd you do it?" she asks in a low voice.

"Kidnapping her was easy. She didn't have as many security guards as imagined," Zaydan says, trying hard not to look away from her piercing eye contact.

"Fingerprints?"

"No ma'am."

"Hmm. Continue," Layla says, her limbs stretched apart on her chair.

"We took her to our place behind the slum. Her hands and legs were tied to a table. We forced pills down her throat. She resisted at first."

"I specifically asked you to deny her death until she begged you for it. Was I not clear?" her voice booms in the halls.

"We, uh… She already had a problem, so… I thought it wouldn't trace back to us… to you,"

Zaydan says, finding it harder and harder to look directly at her.

"I am Layla Malik. Don't forget that," she says, peeling off her many, many masks.

The men finally drop their heads.

"There was something else I ordered you to do," she says, lighting a cigarette. With a slight tilt of her head, she brings the flame to the end. The flicker casts a warm glow to her cold face, illuminating the dark circles around her eyes.

"The hair tie. Yes. You said you wanted her to know why. And she did. That neon hair tie was shoved down her throat along with the pills," Zaydan says, each sentence quicker than the last.

"And then what?" she demands.

"Ma'am, there was a..." Zaydan's associate begins.

"And then, nothing. We made sure she'd OD and then left her on the tracks," Zaydan says, looking at his associate with a warning in his eyes.

"Well then, the debt is paid."

Zaydan and his men are visibly calmer now.

"There's something else, though. That child racket you run... I don't like it." the smoke curls around her lips before she takes a long exhale. The ribbons of smoke dance in the air around them.

"But that's our income..." Zaydan interrupts, and then stops, seeing the mad glint in her eyes.

"I'm sure you'll make the right decision," she says, putting out the cigarette. They stand there, witnessing a daughter filling in her father's shoes. "Leave." She grabs a gin bottle on the table. Gravity of pain is powerful enough to overthrow love. And so, loss sits on the throne, wearing a crown of thorns.

As soon as they leave her place, Zaydan pulls his associate to a corner and puts a gun to his head.

"The fuck were you thinking? The girl is dead, isn't she? Nobody needs to know how."

"She ran because you provided her with a chance to. Just couldn't keep it in your pants, huh, Zaydan?" the associate says, pushing him away.

"Bitch tricked me. But what I don't get is that we ran after her and still couldn't find her. So, how'd she end up dead right under our noses?" Zaydan asks.

"None of our concern anymore. You are right. Let's just… It's better if we shut up okay," the associate says, looking back at the mansion.

15 July 2023
Raphael

And what good did that do her? This question keeps ringing in Raphael's ears ever since he left the cemetery. It pairs well with Amina's screams from the night of the accident.

Raphael walks up to the receptionist at St. Luke's Hospital and says, "Excuse me, I'm here to see the head geriatrician, Dr. Castillo."

After a phone call and a few clicking sounds on a keyboard later... "She'll see you in fifteen minutes. Kindly fill out these forms, Mr. Adler," the receptionist responds.

Twenty minutes after handing in the filled-out forms, Raphael sees a woman in her mid-thirties, walking towards his direction with a stethoscope around her neck; a woman whom he knows all too well.

"Doctor Castillo?"

"It's been a long time, Mr. Adler. I have been meaning to call you."

"Um... how's... how is she?" he asks, his voice faltering intermittently.

"Not great," she responds, touching his shoulder, her eyes downcast.

"But—"

"I left you a message yesterday to come see her. She doesn't remember anybody, Raph. There are variations in her vitals. On top of that, she's refusing to take her medicines."

"Can I see her?" he asks.

"Of course. Follow me."

Annette Castillo used to be Raphael's spouse. Before her, he had another wife, and after her, there was another. But, neither of them had an impact on him like Annette did. She forgave him, proving she is a stronger person than he could ever hope to be. He never wanted her to work, and she wasn't ready to let go of her dreams to feed his male chauvinist ego. So, their marriage eventually fell apart.

The irony that this woman, whom he thought shouldn't be a doctor, is the one taking care of his beloved, dawns on him. He looks at her with admiration in his eyes, thinking if he knew then what he knows now, things would've been a lot different. *And what good did that do her?* Raphael attempts to silence the echo in his head, failing miserably.

Annette leads him to a room and Raphael walks in, his heart racing and palms sweating. There's a woman lying on the bed. He looks at her weak figure, pasty skin, and many new wrinkles around her eyes. He takes the patient's frail, little hand in his own and says, "Mama."

"Oh, baby. My baby!" cries the woman in a white hospital gown. Her eyes well up as she touches his face.

"I'm here, Mama," he says, firmly gripping her.

"I'll leave you two alone," Annette tells them, leaving a mother and her son alone in that bleak hospital room.

"My boy... my beautiful, baby boy!" his mother exclaims in a cracking voice.

"Don't speak, Mama. Just rest," he says, gently brushing her hair.

All of a sudden, she frowns. "Excuse me... Uh. Mmm... Who are you?" she asks, panicking.

"I'm your... your doctor, ma'am," says a heartbroken Raphael, who forces a smile.

"Okay. Is Raphael coming, Doctor? Is my baby here?" she asks him.

Raphael doesn't know what to say. He sits there next to her, a thousand needles pricking his heart.

"I can't sleep. Tell me a story. Will you, Doctor?" she says, handing him a children's book from the side table.

Raphael props the book against the bed with one hand and starts reading as his mother closes her eyes and listens closely with a smile on her face.

As he is nearing the end of the story, he feels her hand become still. He keeps reading. Using his own shivering hand, he tightens his grip. He closes his eyes and finishes the story, "And they lived happily ever after."

The storybook falls to the floor. Dr. Castillo enters the room and sits next to Raphael, holding his hand.

"Annie…" he says before falling on her lap.

She holds him as he cries.

16 July 2023
Aanjaney

Aanjaney is a debased police officer. He has bent more laws than he can remember. Whether it is looking away from a parking violation or embellishing reports or an accident while handling evidence, his corrupt ways have obstructed justice for many innocent people. In the beginning, it was for money. He convinced himself that it was all to make ends meet for his family.

But, his conscience shouts at him, calling him a pretentious liar. Because, he likes doing it. He likes the rush it gives. He used to put those thoughts locked away in a little, black box in his mind, but there are cracks forming in the box now. The carefully bubble-wrapped life that he created is falling apart.

"I told you nothing is going to happen to him if he didn't do anything wrong. He is a minor, and there is a system in place for situations like this," Aanjaney tried to reason with his sister.

He was about to shut his bedroom door when she slammed it open and said, "Oh, fuck your system. You didn't care before. Do I need to wave around a giant wad of money for you to pay attention to me? We are the only two people that know about this, and he doesn't need to get his life tangled in this mess, for his life to be more chaotic than it already is," Ayaana countered.

"You know what, for once in your life, get out of your damn head. Why do you always have to act like a naïve, little fool? So fucking desperate for anything real that you'll latch onto anything sad. For anything to fill the empty shell of a human you are."

The second those words left his mouth, when he saw her standing there, wide eyed and blinking rapidly, her lower lip quivering, that little, black box shook violently inside him.

Now, he is in his office, writing a closure report to be submitted to the Magistrate. He is filing it as another drug abuse case, emphasizing that there are no new leads to pursue.

He decided to do the right thing that felt so wrong to his heart, for his baby sister who he had hurt deeply, for the boy that deserves a chance at life, the chance Evy was denied.

Aanjaney went to the pathologist at St. Luke's hospital in order to persuade them into writing a false report. But, as soon as he saw Linda Mathew in that lab coat, he knew it wouldn't be that hard. He remembered her from school but pretended otherwise. As a matter of fact, he thought it was too easy. But along with his ego, his bank account took the brunt of it, as he transferred the 100000 rupees he promised.

Aanjaney has completed the closure report. He looks at a transparent evidence bag in front of him, containing a neon hair tie. His throat constricts. He loosens the tie around his neck. There is an intense discomfort arising in his stomach, leading to the taste of bile in his mouth. He runs to the bathroom to throw up. The little, black box grows by another few inches.

14 July 2023
3:10 a.m.
Raahil

Raahil waits in the woods until every man of Zaydan Bhai's gang retreats. He looks back and the woman who stood behind him is gone. After picking up a shiny bracelet from the ground and shoving it into his shorts that don't fit right, he starts to look for her. He eventually finds her back at the track, walking around aimlessly, talking gibberish along the way.

Raahil has had many rough days in his life. He has been abused, humiliated, and tortured, but none of that compares to yesterday. He strolled along the streets, looking inside the glass store windows of every shop he passed by. He was nearing Amina's home, and Raahil couldn't wait to make her smile again by telling her about Ayaana and her brother, their big house, and crazy mom.

That's when he saw a woman holding Amina's hand, taking her to a car. He saw another person, a man, putting all her stuff inside the trunk. Raahil ran using all his strength, but by the time he was close, they had already left. He fell on his knees, punching the ground until his knuckles bled. Amina probably left willingly. *Why wouldn't she?* he thought. Both the man and the woman had nice shoes.

Now, when Raahil first sees the woman's face as the train passes by them, he immediately recognizes her. She is the same woman from yesterday; less sparkly and without her shoes. As anger takes hold, Raahil's body becomes an avalanche, ready to unleash the reality of him. His face becomes redder under the moonlight. His narrow eyes, focused on the object of his antipathy. His fist clenches the bottle when he grabs them from his bag.

When the bottle smashes her head, the sound of it makes Raahil's heart race almost as quick as his mind. So, he does it again and again and again. His breath comes in ragged rasps, his voice thick with emotion as he shouts, "Nobody. Takes. Amina. From. Me. Not you. Not her father. Not anyone."

16 July 2023

Ayaana Iyer is sitting on a harbor dock, her jeans pulled up and her legs in the water as she looks at tiny ships in the distance and a group of birds flying home together, in perfect synchronization. While she is enjoying the view, someone sits beside her. She finds her brother giving her his classic lopsided smile.

"Someone, somewhere, is praying for us, without us knowing. How beautiful is that?" she asks.

"Not all of us deserve it, though," he says, looking down at the fish nibbling at his skin.

"True," she replies.

"I am sorry, Ayaana," he says, pausing awkwardly to hold her hand.

"I am sorry too."

They both start laughing soon after.

"Yeah, this was weird," he says.

"Totally. You should've seen your face," she replies, wiping away a runaway tear drop off her face.

Aanjaney grabs a few pebbles and looks at her, his eyebrows raised suggestively.

"Oh, no, no, no," she says.

"C'mon. Let's make a bet then."

"Hmm," she says, stroking her chin.

"If I win, you have to be my assistant for a week."

"Ugh. Fine. But if I win, which I will, you'll set up a dating profile," she says.

"That's not fair. Anyway, I am going to win. So, who cares?" he says, playing with the pebbles in his hand.

"We'll see," she says, grabbing a pebble out of his hand and stretching her arms.

"On three," he begins.

Meanwhile, a few hundred meters away, atop a ship's hatch, a boy carrying an ugly mud-colored bag on his shoulders, is talking to a big man. He notices the scruffy way the man's trousers were tucked into leather boots. He has paintings going up his sleeve too. The shiny pocket watch dangling from his belt sets the boy's skin on fire. The salty wind distracts him temporarily as the feather in the man's hat blows.

"We don't have space for you in our ship, boy."

"Please. I'll do anything. I'll mop the floors every day."

The captain looks up and down the boy, taking in his shabby clothes, the way he stands; trying to make himself appear taller, the little dirt on the side of his forehead and says, "Fine, then. Come aboard. What's your name?" the captain asks.

"Razak," the boy with golden brown skin says, flashing missing front teeth as he smiles.

Aanjaney and Ayaana stand up, pulling their rolled-up jeans back down, laughing out loud. They begin walking on the docks, carrying their shoes in their hands.

"You probably don't remember this, but when you were little, we used to read story books in forts we made."

"Oh, yeah. I remember Fort Iyerland," she says, smiling.

"So, whenever a story was about to be over, you couldn't turn the page. You had this crazy habit of skipping the last chapter because you didn't want the story to end," he says, looking at his little sister.

"What's your point?" she asks him.

"I think it's time to turn the page,'" he says.

"You and I both," she replies.

"Who knows, maybe I'll learn to love again," he wonders aloud.

"Nobody ever needs to 'learn' how to love. We just need to accept and honor the part of ourselves that does know how. Love just is. It is born with us. Just like the stars and oceans and forests, you do not need to justify your existence. You are magic. Be magic."

Simultaneously, on a distant ship, a song is heard;

Six little monkeys jumping on the bed.
One fell off, and bumped his head.
Momma called the doctor and the doctor said,
"No more monkeys jumping on the bed."

THE END

Acknowledgements

To Lea, my Anam kara:
Thank you for seeing me and for the privilege and honor of seeing you.

To Sreevidya, my best-friend/ex-roommate:
Thank you for being my family for the last 8 years.

To Sebin Xavier, my ex-boyfriend:
You were the first person to call me a writer. Thank you for your unending blind faith in me.

To Appu, my little brother:
Thank you for existing. I could not be prouder of the man you are becoming.

To Babu Eapen, my father:
Thank you for showing us how cool it is to be kind. Your strength knows no bounds.

To Bincy Babu, my mother:
Thank you for buying me my first book. I find you in my eyes, my courage, my anger, and my roar.

To Marsh, my friend and keeper: Thank you for teaching me how to breathe.

Author's note

Among the millions of species that inhabit the planet, we are the only one that hunt for hate. Why is that? Since the beginning of time, we have been conditioned to fear differences. This fear evolved into the system that birthed racism, homophobia, sexism, and so much more.

The first step in changing the world is taking pride in our differences. How amazing is it that we speak over seven thousand languages but music means the same everywhere? We exist in different colors and shapes but all our eyes' twinkle when we smile. There is somebody whose breath aligns your own right now, someone, somewhere, whose heart is beating in sync with your own. So, let's not let anybody tell us that differences are to be feared. Let's live and love in our own unique beautiful ways.

Looking at the world as a sad, hopeless place is lazy and limited thinking. I want you to live your lives with wide perspectives. I want us to stitch open wounds, kiss old scars, and treat even the tiniest paper cuts ailing this planet with all the love and compassion we have. Unlike popular belief, it is absolutely possible for one person to change the world.

Kindness works on the principle of chaos theory. Imagine stopping a war by holding the elevator door open for a stranger who desperately needed an act of compassion. You are responsible for the chain reaction you begin. So, go wish your neighbor good morning, plant seeds, donate blood, listen, share your food, rescue animals, compliment someone, and simply smile more.

Treat people like magic until the magic in them remembers. The world is always ready for change, and I am rooting for you.

One day, there will be beauty; unconventional and powerful.
One day, there will be magic; exposed and inviting.
One day, there will be life; entitled to one and all.
One day, there will be love, undefined and glorious.
One day, there will be peace; rightful and free.
One day is yours. It's today, if you want it to be.

Meet the author

Born and raised in India, Sneha Babu is a 25-year-old STEM major, co-founder of a feminist media company by day and author by night. A few years ago, she plotted the trajectory of this story during a discrete mathematics class (there was a flow chart involved). Sneha did not know it then but she had created something that would go on to heal her future self. From trying to solve the climate crisis to smashing patriarchy, her life is an endless rollercoaster of daring dreams.